SO-FMH-706

Table of Contents

Chapter 1 – Amy's Angst

"You might be wondering why I'm so miserable?"

"Um…" Heather muttered. If she were being honest, she hadn't noticed that her bestie wasn't in the best of moods. Amy was eating donuts on her couch and watching chick flicks, but that was something that she loved to do.

Amy sighed and stuffed another donut into her mouth. Heather joined her friend on the couch and gave her a sympathetic look while wracking her brain for what could have caused her such ennui.

"Is this about Miss Marshmallow?" Heather asked, referring to the prissy dog that Amy was caring for after a murder case left the animal without an owner. Amy and her boyfriend Jamie insisted that they were just fostering the dog until a proper forever family could be found for her. However, Heather was not aware of steps that were being taken to find this other home.

Amy liked to complain about how high-maintenance this diva dog could be, but that didn't seem to be what was troubling her today.

"No," Amy said. "She's not actually so bad."

Miss Marshmallow seemed to sense that they were talking about her and rose from her dog bed that Heather couldn't help noticing looked like it had found a permanent location
next to the bookcase. Miss Marshmallow allowed her fur to be pet for a few moments and then decided she wanted her space.

"And she couldn't have put me in a mood like this," Amy continued. "I haven't even showered today."

"Your hair still smells nice," Heather said, trying to compliment her with a silly fact. Amy wrinkled her nose instead of smiling, and Heather tried to think what else could be bothering her. "Is everything all right with Jamie?"

"Of course," Amy said. "He's the perfect boyfriend."

"But do you wish he was more than a boyfriend?" Heather asked. "Do you feel like he's being slow with proposing?"

"No, that's not what's wrong," said Amy, blushing. "And you know how I don't like to rush into things anymore."

"I know," Heather said, looking at the "foster" dog. "So, what's wrong?"

"You know how sometimes when the holidays approach and how being in a tropical paradise should make you happy? And so, if you start to feel sad, it actually makes you feel even sadder because you know that you're supposed to be jolly?" Amy rambled.

"I haven't felt that myself," Heather said. "But I could understand how could be frustrating."

Amy looked at her friend. "You must have been worried about me when I didn't come to Donut Delights today."

"Actually," Heather admitted. "I just assumed that you were helping Jamie with his pet grooming van."

Amy groaned and wrapped herself in a blanket with angry movements. "Well, you know what happens when you assume. You miss that I'm in a state of mourning instead of washing dogs."

"I did come to check on you," Heather said, with just a bit of defensiveness. "And I brought you some of the new flavor of donuts."

Amy emerged from her blankets, finally noticing the box that her bestie was holding.

"You brought the new donuts here?" she asked. "What flavor are they?"

"They're called Spiced Maple Donuts," Heather said, suppressing her smile from growing too large. "Their base is like a spice cake and contains all the favorites: nutmeg, cinnamon, allspice."

"Allspice? Alright, I'm interested," Amy said.

"It's covered in a maple glaze," Heather continued. "To keep it tasting sweet."

"Like maple syrup?" asked Amy. "I love maple syrup. But it is sticky. It's very possible that if I reach my hand into that box to take one that several of them will stick me. I might be forced to take them all."

Heather laughed and offered her the box. "Go ahead."

Amy picked up just two donuts from the box and took a bite. "It's delicious."

"I hope it helps you feel better," Heather said.

Amy took a break from eating her yummy snacks to sigh. "Part of me feels guilty about feeling bad about things too. Because I love these donuts."

"Just tell me what's wrong," Heather said.

"You know how you assumed that because I wasn't at Donut Delights, I was at Jamie's grooming business?" Amy said. "Well, that's what wrong."

"I'm sorry I didn't check on you sooner," Heather started to say.

"No," said Amy. "It's not that assumption. Because you'd normally be right."

"I'm confused."

"Well, now you know how I feel when you solve a case and are too distracted to tell me who the killer is," Amy joked, but then she continued. "I normally am at your donut shop or helping Jamie."

"I thought you loved those two things," said Heather.

"I do," Amy said. "So much! But I just started thinking that everything in my life is based on someone else's thing. I investigate crimes because it's with my best friend and I help with the dogs because it's with my boyfriend. I don't really have my own thing."

"What do you mean?"

"My life is dictated by your murder cases, Jamie's van, and albeit delicious, donuts. I love eating them, but I can't make new recipes like you can. I feel guilty being upset about this because I love so much of my life. But at the same time, I am still upset. I don't have anything that I do that is just mine."

"Do you want to stop working at Donut Delights or being my private investigator partner? You're my best friend. If you want to stop, I'll understand," Heather said.

"No," Amy said. "I don't want to stop. I love these things. And I don't regret moving to Key West to continue being a part of them with you. I just wish I did something that was all my own. Well, besides, hiding under blankets and watching sappy movies."

"Done," said Heather.

"What?"

"It's done," Heather said. "You've got it. Find a job or a hobby that you want to do, and we'll make sure you get the chance to explore it properly. You can still help me with cases and donut testing, but I won't assume you'll always be there. You can do what you need to do for yourself first. And I'm sure Jamie will feel the same way."

"You really are the best best friend," Amy said. "Do you know that?"

"You might have mentioned it to me before," Heather said with a smile. "And I think I also know where you can start."

"What? And where?"

"We've been a bit indecisive this week about where we should go for our Saturday afternoon outing with all our friends," Heather said.

"Why don't you be the one to pick where we go?"

"No pressure," Amy joked. "It just needs to be something fun for seven people, including two seniors and a child."

"It needs to be something that makes you feel like you have your own thing that you can share with your friends," Heather countered.

"Okay," Amy said. "But how should I make this decision? Where should we go on Saturday? And what should I choose my new hobby?"

"I'd love to help you." Heather joked, "But then it wouldn't be your thing."

Chapter 2 – An Artsy Outing

"I like all the flamingoes in this painting," Lilly said.

"Do you like the flamingoes or just that it's very pink?" Heather teased her daughter.

"Maybe both," Lilly admitted with a laugh.

"This was a great idea for an outing," Heather said, turning to Amy.

She had decided that they should check out the art scene in Key West and had visited some galleries in Mallory Square. There were different formats of art including colorful abstract paintings, photography of the ocean, and paintings of sights on the island. Everyone had enjoyed looking at the art, and they all had their favorites.

Lilly liked the animal paintings, while her father Ryan liked the photos. He felt proud when he recognized certain locations on the island, but Heather said he had an unfair advantage. As a detective on the Key West Police Force, he was often traveling around and looking for clues in various places.

Their senior friends Eva and Leila liked an exhibit that they saw featuring photos of ballerinas mid-dance. It was inspiring the two friends to create their own choreography, and they almost knocked over a sculpture of a giant shell.

"Oops," Leila said.

"Maybe we're not meant for high art," Eva laughed.

Jamie seemed to like the paintings with bright colors best, and Amy was keeping her favorites a secret.

"I thought this was something a little different for an outing because it's more about the arts than history or nature," Amy said.

"I like all the trips we go on," Lilly said. "There's so much to do in our new hometown or home island. And the most important thing is that we're all together."

"Someone is definitely on Santa's nice list," Amy whispered in Heather's ear.

"I know," Heather said quietly back. "Luckily, we still have a little time before the holidays are really upon us, so I have time to figure out the perfect gift."

"And the perfect Christmas donut flavor?" Amy asked.

"Yes," Heather said. "I still have a bit of time to figure that out too."

"I'll be happy to sample the possibilities," Amy kindly offered.

"And you're always welcome to help with the donuts," Heather said. "But does this trip mean that you're looking at art as your new hobby?"

Amy nodded. "I used to be involved in it more, and I actually have still been doing some artsy things."

"That's right," Lilly said. "You painted the puppy pictures on Jamie's van."

"And you made the centerpieces at Donut Delights," Heather added.

"That's right," Amy said. "So, I might actually be good at this. It's nice to be reminded because after I decided I should try this, all the wonderful art here has been making me insecure."

"No, you're very talented," Lilly assured her.

Jamie joined them and said, "I was telling her that I'd love to hang up some of her artwork in our house."

Amy shrugged. "I'm going to try it."

"What have we here?" a voice said, coming closer. "I have

finally found the most beautiful works of art in existence."

"Oh, please," Eva said with a slight chuckle.

An older gentleman with a large bowtie approached them. His name was Vincent Valentino, and he had been trying unsuccessfully to woo Eva since they moved in. He kissed Eva's hand, and she called him an "old flirt."

"Did you follow us here because I mentioned that we were going to see some art with our friends today?" asked Eva.

"What?" Vincent asked. "You think I would be so bold as to arrange a forced meeting at a place like this?"

"Yes," Eva and Leila said at the same time.

"You might be right," he said with a twinkle in his eyes. "And there is so much art to see here it took me a long time to find the right gallery."

"I'm sorry you might have wasted your time," Eva said. "We're just about to leave."

"Are you trying to run away from me?" Vincent asked.

"Do you think I would be so coy as to pretend we're leaving someplace in order to tease you?" Eva asked.

"Yes," Leila and Vincent replied at the same time.

Eva shot a glare at her best friend. Leila smiled and then said, "But in this case, she is telling the truth. We were about to head to another art hot spot. Isn't that right, Amy?"

"We've been looking at some of the more established galleries so far today," Amy said. "But there's another place a little more off the beaten path that I'd like to check out. It's a sculpture garden."

"That sounds magnificent," said Vincent.

"I suppose you could join us if you really want to," Eva said. "Seeing as you went to several galleries to try and find us already. But no more kisses on the hand. Or anywhere else."

"You drive a hard bargain," Vincent said, settling for a handshake.

Amy led the way, and they headed towards the sculpture garden.

Garden was a bit of an overstatement. It was a small path that led to a warehouse-like art studio. However, the sculptures and statues that were along this path were impressive. Some were obvious in their likeness to animals or landmarks, and others were more abstract. One looked like a train moving along tracks and about to run into you, while another looked like some sort of mystical bird about to fly away. Some were very tall, and some were closer to Lilly's height.

"I think this is my favorite thing I've seen all day," Amy said, moving closer to a large sculpture. It was abstract but reminded her a flower fighting to bloom. There were also bits of mirror pieces on it that reflected the light in an almost magical way.

"Thank you," a young woman said, walking around the small bend in the path to join them. "I didn't mean to overhear, but that's my piece, and I couldn't help saying something. It's so nice when compliments aren't forced."

"It speaks to me," Amy said. "I can't quite translate what it's saying into English, but I like it."

"Thank you," she said again.

Amy introduced everyone in the group and then the newcomer responded with, "My name is

Kendall Dakwa. I own the building. I would say that I run the studio too, but with all the artistic temperaments that use the space, it doesn't often feel like I'm in charge."

Heather chuckled. Sometimes she felt the same at her donut shop.

"Do a lot of professionals use the space?" Amy asked.

"There are a few sculptors that generally use the studio," Kendall said. "And they're all getting ready for an upcoming contest. But there are people who come here that aren't professionals too. We have several classes in different mediums. In fact, we have a painting class tonight."

"Do you really?" Amy asked.

"And is there space in that class?" Heather asked, smiling at her friend.

"We do," Kendall said. "Are you interested? I'd love to have you join. The more, the merrier. And I have to admit I'd like having a fan in the building."

"I'd love to come," Amy said.

"Let me get you some more information that you can take with you, and I'll have it for you by the time you're finished admiring the garden," Kendall said before leaving for the building.

Amy had a wry grin on her face. "Wow. When I say I'm going to start something new, I really mean it."

Chapter 3 – Master Class

Heather hurried towards the art studio with a box of Spiced Maple Donuts in tow. She was happy that Amy had suggested that they meet up after the class and walk home together. Heather had decided that some donuts from her shop would be a nice touch to bring to the artists. She was hoping that this sweet bribe would allow her a peek at Amy's work-in-progress. She was very excited to see what her friend would create.

Amy waved as Heather entered. Based on the big smile on her face, Heather was confident that her bestie was feeling better about things. The class enjoyed the donuts that Heather offered, and she was allowed a peek at Amy's painting. Even though it wasn't complete, Heather could tell that her friend had a lot of talent. She couldn't wait to see the finished product.

"So, do you think you've found your thing?" Heather asked.

"I've got a good feeling about it," Amy said. "Especially if I'll be treated to donuts after my classes."

"If I can keep seeing your art, it will be a deal," Heather said.

"Great," said Amy. "But we're going to have to start heading out now. The studio is reserved tonight for the professional sculptors who are working on their contest entries."

They were about to leave when Kendall came up to them.

"You didn't tell me how talented she was," Kendall said to Heather. "She has a great eye. And I can say that after seeing her work now, and not just because she liked my work. We might have to put you in a more advanced class."

"I'd be interested in learning some of these other mediums too," Amy said. "I know a bit about painting, but don't know a lot about sculpture. I'd love to learn more. I'll look at the schedule of classes you gave to me."

"I'll do you one better," said Kendall. "You could stay tonight and watch the master sculptors work. That's always inspiring. And then if you'd like to take a class, you'll know what you're in for. Your friend could stay too since she brought us delicious refreshments."

"If that's not infringing on your special thing," Heather said.

"It's fine," Amy said. "This time you're doing my thing with me. It'll be great."

Kendall showed them to some seats around the edge of the studio where they would be able to watch the artists work without getting in their way.

"There are just a few things I should warn you of," Kendall said. "The first is that they are preparing for a competition. They have to make an artistic version of a Christmas tree in 3D. So, this isn't using a chisel and stone type of sculpting. Most of the artists will be combining found parts into their own vision. There will be some metalworking involved and some building. Everyone will have their own technique for the holiday competition."

"It sounds exciting," said Amy.

"What's the other thing you have to warn us about?" Heather asked.

"That the artists might be a bit volatile," Kendall said.

"Thief!" an artist yelled, as she entered the space.

Kendall shrugged. "See what I mean?"

"Kendall," the artist said, running up to her. She had large frizzy hair and huge amounts of original jewelry on.

"What's wrong, Tricia?"

"Somebody robbed me," the artist Tricia said. "That's what's wrong."

"They stole your idea again?" Kendall asked. "Or they stole something else?"

"I had a boat propeller I wanted to use in my design, and it's missing," Tricia fumed.

"Maybe it's just been misplaced?" Kendall suggested.

"It was with all my supplies," Tricia said. "Somebody stole it." The rest of the artists started filling in and listening to the tirade as they got their own work areas set up. There was one other female artist. She was a small woman with a short bob for hair. There were three men that had come in too. One was a giant of a man that was quietly arranging pinecones. A handsome man with big arm muscles was collecting some wires.

The last man decided to insert himself into the argument. He had scraggly hair and was missing a front tooth.

"What is she squawking about?" the man asked. "Is she still going on about last year's competition? Because if she is still saying that I stole her idea, she's crazy."

Kendall began, "Ray, let's not—"

"I was the one who began working with garden trowels long before she did. She stole my idea!" Ray said.

"You see what I have to work with?" Tricia asked. "He stole my idea last year. And now he's still my supplies."

"I didn't steal anything," Ray said.

"Ray, why don't you start working on your entry?" Kendall said. "Tricia, we can look for your propeller together."
"It's a huge propeller. It's not hiding. It's obviously not here. It was stolen," Tricia said. "And now I'm going to have to come up with

an entirely new plan for my tree.
I'm going to be behind schedule."

"If it helps, I can keep the studio
open late tonight," Kendall said.
"I'd have to run home and check
on my dog, but I can keep it open
here."

"I think that will be necessary,"
Tricia said. "If you're going to
allow art thieves to use the space
with me."

Tricia stormed off. Amy turned to
Heather.

"This is going to be an interesting
night," she said.

Chapter 4 – Deadly Decorations

"You're really doing some art classes?" Luz asked. "I think that's wonderful. Perhaps I should explore more artistic ventures myself. I already surprised myself by becoming a donut baker."

Heather smiled at her assistant. She and Amy were at Donut Delights and were making sure that both the Spiced Maple Donuts and her assistants were ready for the day.

Digby leaned on the counter and joined the conversation. "I already have an artistic outlet. I'm going to be in a play."

"That's fitting," Amy said. "You can be rather dramatic."

Digby mimed being shot in the heart by her remark.

"I can't believe how many artists I'm close to," Luz said. "Digby's theater, Amy's painting, and Heather's donuts."

"They are a work of art," Digby agreed. "I loved this new Spiced Maple one, but I guess I do love all of them."

"Thanks," Heather said. "You'll love Amy's art too."
"But don't put it in your mouth," Amy joked.

They all laughed. Amy and Heather then told the others about how they had stayed to watch the sculptors work. The abstract holiday trees that they were making were impressive, but there were definitely big personalities in the room last night.

"Kendall said that I could stop by this afternoon before the watercolors class to look for materials for my own sculpture. I think she wants to mentor me," Amy said. "But I think she also wants me to bring some donuts."

"I can bring some over with you if you want," Heather said. "It's pretty close, and I wouldn't mind taking a walk this afternoon."

"That would be great," Amy said.

Before they could start out though, they had an unexpected visitor in their shop.

"Seasons Greetings," Mr. Rankle called out cheerfully.

Heather and Amy froze and exchanged a look. Mr. Rankle was their shop neighbor that had always despised them for the simple fact that they were from out-of-town. He hated tourists and basically considered everyone who wasn't born on the island to be a tourist. He had given them trouble in the past, not limited to telling customers that their donuts contained food poisoning.

"I know it's a little early," Amy said. "But do you think he was visited by three ghosts last night?"

Heather shrugged. A Scrooge-like experience was as feasible as any other reason for Mr. Rankle's sudden change in behavior towards them.

"Seasons greetings to you too," said Heather.

"Merry early Christmas," Amy added.

Luz and Digby were watching the exchange, waiting to see if the tide would turn and Mr. Rankle would cause trouble. Luz had a hand near the phone, and Digby was debating whether he was willing to sacrifice donuts if hurling them would cause a distraction.

However, Mr. Rankle continued to appear to be a kindly old man. He brought a box of decorations inside with him.

"I couldn't help but notice that your shop was looking a little sparse with Christmas cheer," he said. "So, I brought some extra décor from my shop to help you out."

"That is very kind of you,"
Heather said. However, she
wasn't sure they should accept
the gift in case it turned out to be
some sort of Trojan Horse
dancing Santa. "But I wouldn't
want to put you out and take all
your decorations."

"It's fine. You know that I sell
novelties and so I always end up
with extra decorations at the end
of my season," said Mr. Rankle. "I
want our neighborhood to be
cheery, and so I'll do my part to
make sure it is."

"Thank you," Heather said. "We'll
do our part too."

"Make sure you put them all up," Mr. Rankle said with a sickeningly sweet smile. "Well, happy holidays."

He left them, and they all looked at the decorations confused.

"I don't understand," Amy said. "What's his ulterior motive?"

"Do you think it's possible that he turned over a new leaf and is trying to be a good neighbor?" Heather asked. "Maybe the Christmas spirit got the better of him?"

"No way," Digby said.

Luz nodded, "He did everything he could to try and put you out of business. Why should he stop now?"

"But they're decorations," Heather said. "How can they be part of an evil plot?"

"Use that mind of yours that you use for catching criminals," Digby said. "Maybe he doused it all in cat pee or something gross like that. Then the whole place will stink, and no one will want to buy food."

Heather sniffed the box of decorations. "It smells like holly to me."

"What if it's rigged to catch fire and burn all of poor Donut Delights down?" Luz asked.

Heather looked through the box. "They look like regular lights to me. And I don't think he would stoop to arson. Besides, he likes this building. He just doesn't like us inside it."

"What if there are bugs inside there and they'll crawl out and ruin our ingredients?" Amy suggested.

"No," Luz said, shuddering. "Todo menos eso. Anything but that."

Heather shook her head. "How would Mr. Rankle get those bugs?"

"They're his friends," Amy joked.

"And a bug infestation would hurt the whole neighborhood and not just us," Heather continued.

Luz still looked frightened.

"But if it makes you feel better, we can spray the décor and keep them in airtight bags for a few hours," Heather said. "And then after that time, I guess we should hang them up."
"Are you serious?" Digby asked.

"Yes," said Heather. "If Mr. Rankle is indeed extending the olive branch."

"Which is a pine tree branch this time," Amy said.

"Then I don't want to ignore it," said Heather. "Maybe Christmas makes him jolly, and we can use this festive mood to become better neighbors."

"Well, if you say so," Digby said.

"I do," said Heather. "We'll trust him until there's evidence that we can't. And we'll trust that this new art class is good for Amy."
"Big mistake," Digby muttered. "I mean just about Mr. Rankle."

However, it turned out that he wasn't completely wrong on both counts.

***

"Kendall?" Amy asked as they approached the warehouse studio.

"Are we too early?" Heather asked.

"I don't think so," said Amy. "Maybe a few minutes. But she told me to come in before the class."

They tried the door and found that it was unlocked.

"Oh good. She must be here and expecting us," said Amy.

Heather started to have a bad feeling about what they were walking into, but still followed her friend inside the room.

"Kend-aah!" Amy screamed, after not finishing her mentor's name.

Heather found the light switch and then saw what Amy had seen the outline of. A woman's body had been impaled on the top of one of the tree statues. She was clearly dead, and it was clearly murder.

Chapter 5 – Crime Scene Art

"I'm sorry you had to be the ones to stumble onto this crime scene," Ryan said. "This couldn't have been a pleasant one to find."

Heather responded, "Crime scenes are never pleasant when somebody was murdered."

"It had to be murder, didn't it?" Detective Peters asked. He was Ryan's partner, and while very diligent about his job, was also somewhat new to it.

"I think it had to be," Heather said. "That tree sculpture was over four feet tall, and the victim was impaled right in her abdomen. She couldn't have fallen onto it by accident."

"My face must be as green as the evergreen trees," said Amy. "I feel sick."

"Now what were you two doing here again?" Detective Peters asked. "Or were you just drawn here because you have such a knack for solving cases you're starting to know when they start now?"

"If we could stop a murder before it happened, now that would be a real knack," Heather said. "But it was nothing like that. Amy and I were coming here to see the owner of the building and Amy's new art instructor, Kendall."

"She told us to meet her here," said Amy. "And that's why in the dark, I thought it was her that was killed. I mean, it's still really upsetting that someone else was, but Kendall was becoming my friend."

"Right," Detective Peters said, checking his notes. "The owner is Kendall Dakwa, but the victim is…"

"Tricia Mollins," Ryan answered, being quicker to supply the information than the notebook.

"She was an artist here," Heather said. "We saw her working on her statue for a competition here last night."

"And she wasn't too happy with her fellow artists," Amy said, explaining how Tricia had accused them of theft.

"But if she was the one who was angry with her colleagues, how did that lead to her murder?" Detective Peters asked. "She wasn't the one doing the killing?"

"That guy with the missing tooth was angry too," Amy said. "He accused Tricia of stealing his sculpture idea last year. They both accused each other."

"His name was Ray," Heather added.

"We'll have to speak to him," Ryan said. "And to everyone else who worked with the victim."

"There were four artists her besides Tricia Mollins last night," said Heather. "But I think Kendall would be able to give you more information on them."

"That's something I don't understand," Amy said. "Where was Kendall? She was supposed to meet us here but was late. But why was the door open?"

"She did say that she would let Tricia stay late last night," said

Heather. "But we'll have to get the details on that as well."

"I really hope that Kendall isn't the killer," Amy said. "If she is, everything positive she said about my art could have been a lie."

"You're a great artist and a great investigator," Heather said. "No matter how this case turns out, both of those things will be true."

"Thanks," Amy said.

"Did all of the artists who were here last night hear that Kendall said she would let Tricia use the space last night?" asked Ryan.

"Yes," said Heather. "She made an offer at the end of the session for others to stay too if they wanted to work on their projects some more. I'm not sure if any of them took her up on the offer."

"They might have come back later to commit the crime too," said Amy.

"But how did they commit the crime?" Detective Peters said, looking at the crime scene. The body and the top of the sculpture had been removed so that the medical examiner could conduct an autopsy, but the bottom half of the statue remained.

"That is a good question," Heather said. "We already determined that Tricia Mollins couldn't have fallen onto the tip of the statue."

"And it was a very pointy," Amy said. "You don't often realize how dangerous the tip of a Christmas tree can be."

"Well, it's not often that the tree is made out of pipes," said Heather. "And it was a work in progress, so I think the jagged part at the top would have eventually been softened."

"Whose art project was this?" Ryan asked.

"I think it was that big quiet guy's," Amy said.

"I believe his name was Horatio," Heather said. "But he definitely was a quiet man. I think we maybe heard two words from him in the entire time that everyone was working."

Ryan nodded. They continued to look at the setup of the room. It was still arranged with the sculptures taking up a large section in the middle of the room. The statute made by the quiet man was made out of pipes and tubing, with pinecone accents. Next to his was a very tall tree made out of pinwheels and lights that was being worked on by the small woman in the class. Continuing in a circle around the room, next was the handsome man's metal tree. Ray's tree came after that. It was still in rough shape but was being decorated with fishing lure. Finally, was Tricia's own tree. It looked as if at first it was being built from material scavenged from boats, was being changed to include other tools as well.

"I hate that something that's supposed to be so creative and cheery was used to kill someone," Amy said.

"It might have been difficult to kill someone too," Heather said. "As Detective Peters pointed out if she couldn't have fallen on it, then someone had to drop her onto the murder weapon."

"Like someone picked her up and dropped her on it?" Amy asked.

"Or threw her," said Heather.

"Are any of the artists strong enough to have done that?" asked Ryan.

"I think any of the men could have. They all looked pretty strong," said Heather. "Kendall also has big arm muscles from her work."

"I really hope it's not her," Amy said.

"Is there any other way that she could have gotten on top of that tree statue?" Detective Peters asked.

"There's always the chance of other possibilities," Heather said. "But I don't see any stepstools or ladders in here. Do you?"

"No," Peters said. "Though I can keep looking."

"If the killer didn't have any help, then it had to be someone strong," Ryan said, thinking.

"Is there anything else you found that could be helpful?" Heather asked.

"Unfortunately, because so many people use this space, there are too many fingerprints o be of any use," said Ryan. "But there is something interesting over here."

He gestured to a can of spilled paint on the ground.

"Was this like this yesterday?"

"No," said Heather. "It must have spilled last night."

"Are you thinking what I'm thinking?" Amy asked, looking at the reddish paint on the ground.

"What?" asked Heather. "That the killer might have gotten some of the paint on him last night."

"Right," said Amy. "So, there's a chance that we might be able to catch him red-handed."

They all groaned, but secretly hoped she was right.

Chapter 6 – Questioning Kendall

"I didn't know you were private investigators too," Kendall said.

"They've helped us on several cases," Ryan said, proudly. "And this seems like an especially vicious case."

"I can't believe someone was killed in my studio," Kendall said. "Poor Tricia."

Kendall sat on one side of the table in the interrogation room at the police station, while the two detectives and Amy and Heather were on the other.

"Why didn't you meet me today?" Amy asked. "Where were you?"

"I'm sorry," Kendall said. "I was just running late. I have a new dog, and he's been pretty hyper. By the time I got to the studio, it was already marked off as a crime scene. I'm just glad I got there before the watercolor class showed up. I'm sure this scared off some of the students."

"Miss Dakwa, we need to know more about your studio space," Ryan said.

"Sure," said Kendall. "What do you want to know?"

"Who had access to the building?" Heather asked.

"I'm the only one with keys," Kendall said. "But I sometimes let people stay in the building when I'm not there. I make sure to open up for classes and for studio time. If I know them well, sometimes I let people close up for me too."

"And what were the circumstances last night?" Ryan asked.

"We had the studio open for the sculptors to work on their entries for the tree statue competition, but Tricia was upset about her materials being missing, and I told her that she could stay late. I gave the same offer to all the other artists so it would be fair."

"And who did stay?" Detective Peters asked.

"Tricia and Horatio were the ones who stayed late," Kendall said. "But Tricia was there by herself when I left."

"You left her alone?" Heather asked.

"Yes," said Kendall. "I trusted her in the workspace, and she told me that she would lock the doors when she left."

"What time was that?" Heather asked.

"I must have left around nine," said Kendall. "I had to go home and let the dog out."

"Did you ever have any troubles with Miss Mollins?" Ryan asked.

"She could be a bit of a handful," Kendall admitted. "But I wouldn't call it real troubles."

"Because it does seem like you were the last one to see her alive," Ryan said. "Besides her killer. Unless, of course, you were the killer too."

Kendall paled, but then said, "I didn't kill her. There was no reason for me to kill her."

"Maybe she took advantage of your studio a little too often?" suggested Ryan. "Or she needed more attention than you wanted to give?"

"No," Kendall said. "Many artists are a little strange or demanding. And she was one of my best artists. She won the tree competition last year, and that made many students sign up for classes with me."

"Do you know anyone who would want to hurt her?" Heather asked.

"Like Ray?" asked Amy.

"Tricia and Ray were at odds because of the competition last year and, as you saw, she thought he was the one to take her boat propeller. She would have little tiffs with most of the other artists at one point or another. There wasn't anything that I thought would lead to killing her," Kendall said.

"Unfortunately, something did," said Ryan.

"Is this a high stakes tree sculpting competition?" Detective Peters asked. "Would winning it be something to kill for?"

"It's more of a pride thing than the prizes offered," said Kendall. "I also wouldn't have thought it could lead to murder. But obviously, something did."

"Did anyone else know she would be there that night?" Heather asked. "Besides the other artists."

"I don't know," Kendall said. "It was a bit late when the session ended. I know Lincoln had to run away right when the regular time let out. And I think the others headed home. They might have told someone she was there, but it doesn't give anyone a lot of time to plan to get there. I didn't see her use her phone to let anyone know she was staying late. I don't know who she would have called. She lived alone, and I don't know of her being romantically involved with anyone."

"Anyone besides the artists wouldn't have known about the pointy statue perfect for killing," said Amy. "But, then again, they might not have planned this too far in advance. Maybe they just saw the opportunity to kill and took it."

"There were no other signs of a struggle beside the paint can," said Heather. "So, either she was caught by surprise or didn't feel threatened by the killer."

"Was there anything special about this paint can found at the scene?" Ryan asked, showing

Kendall a picture the color, and giving Amy a warning look to tell her not to repeat her joke from before.

"We have a lot of paint in the studio," Kendall started before looking at the photo. "Actually, there is something about that. That's a custom-ordered color. It's not one you'd find everywhere."

"It looks red to me," Detective Peters, said frowning.

"It's called Holly Berry Jam Red," said Kendall. "Ray had ordered it for his project. It arrived yesterday, but I don't think I saw him open it while I was there."

"So, how did it get on the floor?" Amy asked. "Was there an art thief that was using paint and propellers? Or did it fall during the commission of the crime? Or was it some sort of modern art project on the floor and a murder just happened to occur near it?"

Ryan started to thank Kendall for her help with the matter and told her they would contact her if they had any other questions. He also mentioned that they would be checking up on her timeframe and alibi to make sure that she couldn't have returned to the studio that night.

"Wait a moment," Kendall said. "I guess I can't account for all of the night, but I do have some timestamps for part of it. I was taking pictures of my new puppy on my phone and the time is on them."

She showed the investigators her phone, and they saw many pictures throughout the night of an adorable sandy furball completely destroying her living room.

"Miss Marshmallow really isn't that bad," Amy said to her friend.

"The only one who is really bad in this case is the killer," said Heather. "And we need to figure out who that is."

"Right," said Amy. "Whoever decided to decorate the tree in such a terrible way needs to go to jail."

Chapter 7 – Lights

After the decorations from Mr. Rankle had been found to be bug-free, Heather's team began making Donut Delights look more festive.

"Maybe he really does just want our whole street to look jolly," Amy said, not sure if she believed it or not.

"We were looking a little bare," Heather said. "Because the shop still feels so new, I haven't been doing very much to furnish it for the holidays. I was still getting used to the regular look of it."

"Are you getting used to the employees too?" Digby asked.

"You do take some getting used to," Amy teased.

They laughed and began putting up the decorations that had been donated to them.

"I'm sorry that a murder case is interfering with your new hobby," Heather said.

Amy shrugged. "It is what it is. I still want to continue with the art. I think the best thing for us to do is to catch this killer quickly."

"I'd love to do that," Heather said. "We have a lot of artists that we're going to have to interview."

"Almost all of them seem like they had the opportunity to pull it off," said Amy.

Heather nodded. "They all knew that she would be working late that night. One of the artists could have come back later in the evening and pretended that they wanted to work on their own project. But what they really wanted was the time alone with Tricia Mollins to murder her."

"They also all knew about the current state of the statues," said Amy. "They knew that Horatio's was pointy enough to cause damage. But that it was short enough for it to be used as a weapon."

"This lady was really impaled by a tree?" Digby asked.

"It was a metal statue made of pipes," Heather explained.

"And it was like those pits you see in movies," Amy continued. "Where you fall through the floor and onto a spear."

"Yuck," said Digby. "And you think she fell through the floor?"

"Actually, we think that someone strong threw her onto it," Heather said.

"I hate killers," Luz said, joining them. "They're so mean."

"Agreed," said Amy. "The problem is that we still have a lot of suspects."

"Right," said Heather. "It was Horatio's statue that was used, and he was the last artist to leave besides Tricia that night. The paint on the floor was Ray's, and he was the one who fought with the victim that morning. The other man--"

"The handsome guy," Amy said, nodding.

"He would also have been strong enough to have killed her," Heather continued. "And the female artist, Lucy, also knew Tricia would be there that night."

"I like that you're not including Kendall in this list," Amy said.

"It is possible she did it," said Heather. "But those photos do show that she was at home a good portion of the night, and it does seem like her business might suffer because of the murder. Right now, there's no motive for her to commit the crime."

"And I hope it stays that way," Amy said.

They finished setting up the decorations and admired their handiwork.

"This looks festive and cheerful," Heather said. "Good job, everyone."

"There sure are a lot of lights though," said Amy.

"Bright and cheerful," Heather amended.

"Merry Christmas!" Mr. Rankle said, entering the shop.

"Merry Christmas," Heather said. "Did you come to admire our display based on your contributions?"

"Even better," Mr. Rankle said. "I came to bring even more holiday cheer."

He presented them with another box of decorations.

"Thank you," Heather said. "But I think we've decorated the shop as much as we can. It's already lovely based on what you gave us before."

"I know that you're new to the Christmas season here," Mr. Rankle said. "And that's why I'm going out of my way to help you out. You see, because we're so tropical and are surrounded by palm trees, sometimes people don't think of the holidays as really being upon us. And so, we as a neighborhood need to do our part to make it as festive as possible."

"Okay," Heather said. "I guess we'll do our part for the neighborhood."

"How many decorations do you have up?" Amy asked suspiciously.

"See for yourself," said Mr. Rankle. "I have those snowy paintings on my windows and a winter train display setup. I would put up the twinkle lights, but unfortunately, they bother my old eyes. I wouldn't want them to go to waste though, and that is why I'm donating them to you."

Heather thanked him for his new contribution and then turned to her staff after he left.

"His behavior is confusing," said Heather. "But he does have decorations up himself."

Digby shrugged. "The last restaurant I worked at on this street put up lights for the holidays. They didn't go crazy though because they wanted the possibility of a romantic atmosphere."

"Do you think he's trying to lull us into a false sense of security?" Amy asked. 'The first batch of decorations were okay, but he did something tricky with these ones?"

"Let's take the same precautions as before," Heather said. "I really

don't want to be worried about
Christmas lights when I have a
killer to track down."

Chapter 8 – The First Artist Interview

Heather and Amy approached a bright little house with a mosaic driveway and pinwheels in the yard. They knocked on the door and waited for the female artist from the sculpting session to answer.

"Hello?" the small woman said.

"You're Lucy Long?" Heather asked.

"Yes," she said. "I remember you. You were the beginner artists watching us work the other night."

"Well, I'm an artist," Amy said happily. "And she's my friend."

"We're also private investigators," Heather said. "We're assisting the Key West police on a murder case."

"A murder case?" Lucy asked. "Was it someone I knew?"

"Tricia Mollins," Heather said. "We'd like to ask you some questions."

"Sure," Lucy said, leading them inside. "I can't believe Tricia is dead."

They sat down in her living room, and Amy took out her tablet to take notes on their questioning.

"Did you know Tricia Mollins well?" Heather asked once they were all situated.

"You get to know the other artists at the studio," Lucy said. "I didn't hang out with her outside of the art sessions, and I'm not sure if any of the others did. She could be overwhelming at times. But she was working there for a few years."

"She might not have been friends with any of the others, but did she have any real troubles with anyone there?" Heather asked. "Well," Lucy said, biting her lip. "She and Ray were at odds a lot."

"That's who we saw her fighting with about stealing each other's ideas?" Amy said.

"That's right. They were arguing while you were there," Lucy said. "And that was mild for them. When the competition rolled around last year, they were screaming at each other daily. They both said that the other one stole their idea for the competition."

"Did one of them do it?" Heather asked.

Lucy shrugged. "They ended up with similarly themed pieces, so I think one did borrow ideas from the other. I couldn't say who had the idea first."

"But if one of them thought that they were wronged by the other it could be a motive for murder," Amy said.

"If you were really worried about secrecy for the contest, then you should make your own arrangements for design. Most of the time we work in the same space, so you're bound to see some of what the others are working on. Most of the time it's fun. It can be inspiring," said Lucy.
"Do the others feel the same?" Heather asked.

Lucy shrugged. "I think Lincoln found the atmosphere inspiring too. He was easy to get along with. Horatio was too. He was quiet. But Ray was quite volatile. Maybe being there and being angry helped him with his art."

Amy raised her eyebrows.

"Did you stay to work on your sculpture after the session that night?" Heather asked.

"No," Lucy said. "I didn't run out of there as quickly as Lincoln did. He had band practice. He's there all night after the sessions. But I did leave soon after the regular time. I think only Horatio and

Kendall were still there with Tricia when I left."

"And what did you do after you left?" asked Heather.

"I just went home," Lucy said. "Nothing exciting."

"Were you alone?" asked Heather.

A flicker of annoyance passed over Lucy's face, but then she said, "That's right. This is a small place, and I live here alone. I'm not seeing anyone at the moment."

"So, no one can verify what time you were here?" Heather asked.

"I was home alone watching TV," Lucy said. "I could tell you what I was watching, and you could compare it to the times it was on. I was watching this comedy about a dysfunctional family, and in this episode, the wife was angry at the husband again—"

"That's all right," Heather said, stopping her. "We appreciate the attempt."

"And the spoilers," said Amy.

"But nowadays all recaps of shows can be found easily. It doesn't prove you were home watching it at the time," said Heather.

"Oh," Lucy said, disappointed. "But I hope you're not considering me a real suspect. I always got along with Tricia. And I didn't care about the tree sculpture contest like some of the others did. I was just building for fun."

"Was the tree contest extremely competitive?" Heather asked.

"For some people," said Lucy. "Like for Ray. He really wanted to win. If it's not in bad taste to use the phrase, I'd say he'd kill to win it."

Chapter 9 – A Ray of Suspicion

After their talk with Lucy, Heather
and Amy were eager to talk with
Ray about his feud with Tricia
and how badly he wanted to win
the holiday tree competition.

"It really sounds like it's him so
far," Amy said. "Do you think it's
possible that we could figure out
who the killer is so quickly?"

"It's been a strange season all
around. After all, Mr. Rankle has
been surprisingly kind," said
Heather. "Maybe we will catch a
break with this case. But let's not
get ahead of ourselves. Let's
hear what Ray has to say about
that night."

Amy nodded. "But I like that it doesn't seem as though Kendall did it, or Lucy."

"Lucy has a weaker alibi than Kendall," Heather said, thinking about it. "But she's also the smallest artist there. I don't think she could have physically thrown Tricia Mollins so that she would have landed on the unfinished tree tip."

"Good point," Amy said, before cringing at her own pun.

They arrived at Ray's house that should by any rational standard really be called a shack. However, because it was by the ocean, it didn't seem as lousy a

place to live as the slanted walls
might have suggested.

There were several large pieces
in the front yard that could either
have been junk or art. Heather
wanted to ask her friend what she
thought of them but didn't want to
insult the suspect before they got
to ask him any questions about
the murder.

Ray saw them coming and
stomped on to his porch. His hair
looked more unkempt than usual,
and he was scowling.

"I thought you might be
customers wanting to buy some
of my statues, but you're those
amateurs from our tree building

session," Ray said. "You're probably just here to see what gossip you can find out about the murder."

"We are here about the murder," Heather said. "But not as curiosity seekers. We're actually private detectives, and we're helping the police on the case."

"They can't solve it on their own?" Ray asked with a sneer.

"They thought that because we were there earlier on the night that Tricia Mollins was killed that we might be able to offer some insight and help the case get closed sooner," said Heather, evenly. "I think we can all agree that we'd like to see the killer behind bars as soon as possible."

"I guess you're right about that," Ray admitted. "I hated Tricia as much as the next person, but being a killer is worse than being a thief. Whoever did this is much worse than Tricia was."

"You see," Amy started. "You already admitted that you hated her. That seems suspicious."

"She gave me reason to dislike her," Ray said. "I ain't gonna lie about it. Besides, I'm sure all the other artists knew it anyway."

"She accused you of stealing her materials and her idea last year," Heather said.

"I didn't take anything of hers," he said defensively. "If she can't keep track of her own materials, that's her fault. And I didn't steal her idea. She stole mine! She just made a bigger stink about it to try and cover up what she did."

"I guess this contest is pretty important to you?" Heather asked.

"It's the principle of it," Ray said. "I should have won last year, and I didn't. I wanted to win this year."

"I suppose with Tricia out of the running, now it will be easier for you to win?" Heather suggested.

"No," Ray said. "I mean, probably yeah. But that's not how I wanted it. I wanted to rub her face in the loss."

"Suspicious again," Amy commented.

"Last year she stole my tree idea with the trowels and garden tools for materials. Then, she accuses me of stealing her idea, when it was really mine. And then she won anyway, even though she was a thief. I wanted to beat her at her own game."

"Are you sure you didn't settle for making her a permanent Christmas ornament?" Amy asked.

"No," Ray said. "I didn't kill her."

"What did you do after you left the studio last night?" Heather asked.

"I went out for a few drinks," Ray said.

"Where was that?" asked Heather.

"A few places here and there," said Ray.

"Do these places have names?" Amy asked, her patience wearing thin.

"I can't remember," Ray said. "I was annoyed after working and just wanted to relax. I walked around to different bars, and by the end of the night, I couldn't say where I was."

"Could one of those places you wandered have been back to the studio?" Heather asked.

"No," Ray said. "I didn't go back that night. I promise."

"Yeah. We'll just take you at your word," Amy said.

"Look, I'm having a bad enough day as it is without being accused of murder," Ray said. "My favorite shoes have been missing, and I have to wear these ones that are slightly too small. And I burned my breakfast. And I don't know when we'll be allowed back in the studio because Tricia went and got herself killed."

"Well, thank you for your time," Heather said. "We'll be in touch if we have any more questions."

"Fine," Ray said. He walked back into his house, grumbling as he had to walk in his shrunken shoes.

Heather and Amy started to walk away from the house.

"He has prime suspect written all over his face," Amy said.

Heather nodded. "We still need to talk to the others, but he didn't do anything to make himself looks less guilty. He had no alibi to speak of and hated the victim."

"He wasn't shy about saying that either."

Heather paused. She took a closer look at one of the piles of metal in his front yard.

"And there's something else to make him look like he did it."

"What's that?" asked Amy.

"What did Tricia say was stolen from her?"

"Besides her ideas?" Amy said, thinking. "A propeller."

Heather pointed at something hiding in the pile of metal. It was a boat propeller.

"Just like that one," Heather said.

Chapter 10 – The Judge

"It was just sitting in his yard?" Ryan asked.

"Well, it was part of a piece of art," Amy said. "You needed to look for it."

Ryan exhaled. "That does make him look more suspicious."

"You're the artist," Heather said, turning to her friend. "But that piece looked to me like it was hastily thrown together."

Amy nodded. "Some of the paint was still wet, but if it was kept outside, it might have taken over a day to dry."

"It definitely looks like he took her propeller," Heather said. "But does that have anything to do with her murder? Or was his theft his revenge for what happened last year?"

"Peters and I will talk to him again, and we'll analyze the propeller more. If we could prove in court that it was the victim's, it could help our case," said Ryan.

"But the propeller was missing before the murder," Heather reminded them. "That was what started Tricia's accusations that night."

"And maybe that's what caused Ray to snap," Amy said.

"Maybe," said Heather. "Did you and Peters find out anything else that could be helpful?"

She faced her husband. They were all at the police station discussing the case, and looking wistfully at the now empty box that used to contain Spiced Maple Donuts.

"The medical examiner gave us the results of the autopsy. The cause of death was what we expected, but he was able to narrow the timeframe that attack happened to between ten and midnight."

"I think Kendall's photos with her dog were during that window of time," Heather said. "So, if it helps us eliminate one suspect, that was helpful news already."

"Unfortunately, it's the only clue that narrows things down," said Ryan. "We've been checking fingerprints found at the crime scene, but there are so many of them in the space. They must be from many artists that have been there before. And other artists could have used gloves."

"The killer too," said Amy.

"Was there any DNA at the scene?" asked Heather.

"It's the same situation as the fingerprints," said Ryan. "There were many hairs found at the scene, but they could have been there before the murder. We checked the victim's clothes for clues and came up short. Unfortunately, there was no evidence under her fingernails either."

"Which further makes me think that the attack came as a surprise," said Heather. "She didn't have a good opportunity to fight back."

It was if there was a collective sigh from the group. They knew that they needed to find some more clues to crack the case, and they were out of donuts.

Luckily, Detective Peters came in at that time with some good news.

"I found her," Peters said, grinning.

"Who's her?" asked Amy. "Is it the killer? Is it really a her? Tell me it's not Kendall."

"I didn't find the killer. At least not yet," said Peters. "But I did find the founder and head judge of the Key West Holiday Tree Sculpture Contest, or K.W.H.T.S.C."

"That's not a great abbreviation," Amy said.

Peters nodded, but then said, "But maybe she could shed some light on the competition, and we could see if it contributed to a motive to murder."

"Is she coming in?" Ryan asked.

"She's parking her car now," Peters said. "She should be in any minute."

"Now, I really wish I had more donuts," Heather said.

"I was already wishing that," said Amy.

An older woman entered the station. Her hair was decidedly set in place at the proper curl that she liked, and even though it was still hot outside, she had a fur wrap draped around her shoulders,

"Ms. Wenderly, thank you for coming in," Peters said, leading her over to the group. "This is my partner, Detective Shepherd."

"Charmed," she replied.

"And this is my wife Heather, and her investigative partner Amy. They consult with us on cases from time to time," Ryan said.

"That sounds so exciting," Ms. Wenderly said. "I'm always looking for something exciting to be a part of. That's one reason why I began the K.W.H.T.S.C."

"Right," Amy said. "You didn't want to include a word beginning with a vowel in that title? Make it a little more palatable like S.C.U.B.A.?"

"What's wrong with K.W.H.T.S.C.?" Ms. Wenderly asked.

"Nothing," Ryan said quickly. "We'd just like to learn more about it."

"Yes," Heather said. "What was the other reason that you began it?"

"Pardon?" Ms. Wenderly asked, still distracted by the insult to her contest's name.

"You said excitement was one reason for the contest. What's the other reason?" asked Heather.

"You don't miss a beat," Ms. Wenderly complimented her and turned her back to Amy. "I did it to make the island more festive. I'm originally from the Northwest, and I was always covered in snow around the holidays. It didn't seem quite right to be able to be surrounded by palm trees for Christmas, and so I started this art competition to add some more décor. I love supporting the arts, and this allows for a lovely festive display for people to look at."

"We're afraid that one of the participants in this competition has been killed," said Ryan.

"Detective Peters mentioned that," Ms. Wenderly said, frowning. "Do you think it's possible it has something to do with the contest?"

"That's what we'd like to find out," Ryan said.

"What's the grand prize?" Heather asked.

"It's five hundred dollars," Ms. Wenderly said. "It's not nothing, but I'm not sure it's something to kill for. Depending on the materials they choose to use, some artists might spend close to that on their statue. Of course, others are more resourceful and find inexpensive ways to make beautiful art. I always thought that artists were more in it for the pride than for the prize."

"Pride might have been a motive," Amy said. "We just saw a sample of the emotions the artists were feeling the night before the murder."

Ms. Wenderly didn't turn to face Amy, but did respond with, "I wanted to inspire good and beauty with this contest. I wouldn't like to think it led to this horror."

"Would someone have wanted to stop Tricia Mollins from winning a second year in a row?" Heather asked.

"Quite possibly," said Ms. Wenderly. "But I would have thought that they would have done it with their art."

"Do you remember an entry last year that was similar to Tricia's?" asked Heather.

"Yes, actually," said the older woman. "There was another garden tool themed tree, but it wasn't as fully realized as hers. In fact, it helped to convince me of the genius of simplicity of her design. She used the tools of gardening to create something that should have come from a garden."

"That does sound like a nice art piece," said Amy.

Ms. Wenderly allowed her a look. "It really was."

"And you're the judge of this contest?" Ryan asked for clarification.

"I'm the head judge, but I have two other helpers," she said. "It helps to keep things more balanced."

They thanked her for her help
and were about to send her on
her way when Ms. Wenderly
offered one more helpful tidbit.

"I'm not sure if there are still
pictures of the prize winner, but
Tricia Mollins did make some
lovely small-scale models for
tourists to buy. Apparently, after
winning the contest, she did quite
well with her Christmas business
from selling them."

"So, there still could be a motive
for killing to win the contest,"
Heather said after she left.

"Right," said Amy. "It helped her
to sell her art and increase her
business."

"And money is always a motive for murder," said Heather.

Chapter 11 – Another Artist

"I'm Heather Shepherd, and this is Amy Givens. We're private investigators, looking into the murder of Tricia Mollins. Do you mind if we ask you some questions?"

Horatio looked at them but didn't say anything. He leaned on his doorframe, considering it.

"We're trying to catch a killer," Amy said, trying to keep her temper. "And we need some more information to do it."

"We really would appreciate your help," Heather said.

"You can either talk to us or the police," Amy said. "But if you don't talk to us, it does look like you're hiding something."

Horatio still didn't say anything, but he held the door open for them to come inside his house. He led them to his kitchen table where there were enough seats for them all to sit down, comfortably. The table was covered with art supplies rather than food.

"Thank you," Heather said. "First, I'd like to ask you if you knew Tricia Mollins well?"

Horatio shook his head, and finally answered, "Just studio."

Amy looked at her friend. "Do we have another Geoff Lawless on our hands?" she asked, referring to Jamie's old boss, who was another large man of few words.

"And did you get along with her?" Heather asked.

Horatio nodded.

"We'd like to talk to you about your artwork," Heather said.

"Destroyed," Horatio said, quietly.

"Yes," Heather said, suddenly feeling a slight pang of sorrow for the man after seeing his expression. "Unfortunately, the police did have to disassemble the piece in order to move the body."

"It was supposed to be good," he said. "Not for that."

"Why did you decide to use sharp pipes like that for your piece?" Heather asked.

Horatio stood up and looked around the room. He scanned his pile of sketchbooks and then picked one up. He opened it to a drawing and showed them. The sketch was of several pipes intertwining to form a star.

"This was what you were planning on making?" Heather asked.

Horatio nodded.

"It's beautiful," Amy said. "I love how all the pieces come together."

He looked down, clearly having mixed emotions about how the piece could have looked and what became of the work-in-progress.

"We heard that you stayed late at the studio," Heather said. "You and Tricia were the only artists to do so."

"She and Kendall were alive when I left," he said. "Didn't know it would happen."

"What time was that?"

"Eight-thirty. Around," he said.

"Honey, what's going on?" a woman asked, coming into the room.

"Police," he said.

"Well, private investigators working with the police," Amy said. "But close enough."

"Wife," he said to them. "Halina."

"I hope you're not grilling my husband," she said. "He doesn't like to talk much."

"We're not trying to inconvenience anyone," Heather said. "But we are trying to solve a murder. Your husband's sculpture was used the murder weapon, and he was one of the last people to leave the studio that night."

"But he was home by nine thirty," his wife said. "And then he was with me the rest of the night. He couldn't have been involved in any murder."

"He was home by nine thirty?" Heather asked. "You said that you left at eight thirty. It doesn't take an hour to get from the studio to your house. What were you doing at that time?"

"Nothing deadly or sinister," Halina said. "Horatio is the kindest man you'll ever meet. He's just a big guy, so some people find him intimidating. But he's not a killer."

Horatio stopped scanning another pile of notebooks and presented another picture to the investigators. They were sketches of the stars.

"You were drawing these on your way home?" Heather asked.

Horatio nodded. Heather was inclined to believe him, and if his wife were telling the truth, then he would have been at home at the time the murder occurred.

"Do you know anyone who would want to do this to Tricia Mollins?" Heather asked.

Horatio shook his head, and Halina picked up the slack in the conversation, "She could be loud and dramatic, but it wasn't worth killing over. I know that Ray guy was obsessing over the competition, but he also got real squeamish the day that you cut your arm. I don't think he does well with blood. He wouldn't have like to kill somebody in a messy way, and if you said Horatio's statue was the murder weapon, I assume it was messy."

"Did you go to the studio a lot?" Heather asked.

"I like to watch my husband work and to bring him snacks," Halina said. "But I work nights too, so I can't come all the time. Hey, maybe it was Tricia's boyfriend that killed her."

"What do you mean?" Heather asked.

"I mean that I never see her boyfriend bringing her snacks. Maybe it wasn't that serious," Halina said. "And maybe he did kill her. I wouldn't have thought so at first, but it's usually spouses and significant others that commit the crimes, isn't it? What a depressing statistic."

"Who was her boyfriend?" Heather asked. "No one else mentioned her having one."

"They were probably trying to keep it quiet then," said Halina. "But they forget that just because Horatio is quiet, doesn't mean that he can't hear."

"And what did Horatio hear?"

"That Tricia was at least sleeping with, if not dating, the other artist there, Lincoln."

Horatio nodded.

"Thank you for telling us," Heather said. "I think it's time we spoke to him."

Chapter 12 – Lincoln Lover?

"I don't know what you're talking about," Lincoln said after Heather and Amy introduced themselves and asked about his relationship with Tricia Mollins. He crossed his muscular arms across his chest.

"Maybe he'd prefer to discuss this down at the station?" Amy suggested.

"I could call Detective Shepherd," Heather said, taking her cell phone.

"No," Lincoln relented. "That won't be necessary. I guess I'll talk to you. I just don't want to get all wrapped up in this murder when it has nothing to do with me."

"You weren't seeing the victim?" Heather asked.

"Who told you I was?" he asked.

"A witness who is willing to testify about romantic comments that were heard exchanged between you and Tricia Mollins," Heather said. "Did he get it wrong?"

"Look, yeah, okay," he rambled. "Tricia and I were seeing each other. But it was casual. We weren't planning on getting married or anything. We were just having some fun."

"But you wanted to keep it a secret at the studio?" Heather asked.

"I didn't want to advertise it," Lincoln said. "I don't mean to be vain, but I probably could have found a more attractive girlfriend."

"Can we arrest him now?" Amy asked.

"Tricia was a great artist, and she had some good qualities, but I wasn't serious about her. But I'm so busy in my life that I don't have the time to go out and find the person I really want. And I was tired of one night stands. Tricia was too. And so, in that respect we were perfect for each other," Lincoln said.

"Seriously," said Amy. "Do we have some cuffs?"

"What are you so busy with besides sculpting?" asked Heather.

"I'm in a band," Lincoln said.

"Of course!" said Amy with distaste.

"Maybe you've heard of us? Lincoln and the Loggers?"

"Can't say we have," Heather said. "Now, where we you the night of the murder? Where did you go when you finished the group session at the studio?"

"Around what time?" he asked.

"Between ten and midnight," said Heather.

He groaned. "I guess I almost had a perfect alibi. I had band practice that night, and the whole group was there. With the friends watching us, there were about a dozen people there. I headed right over after the sculpting session to make it on time. And the thing is, we normally rock out until one or two a.m."

"But you didn't that night?" prompted Heather.

"No," Lincoln said. "Maplehead Mike was sick and had to go home early. We couldn't practice anymore without him. Nobody else could keep time on the drums. And even after I talked with some friends for a while, I was still out of there before eleven."

"And where did you go?" Heather asked.

"I wandered around for a while to clear my head because I was really bummed that we didn't get to practice," Lincoln said. "And then I headed home."

"Alone?"

"Yeah," Lincoln said. "I knew Tricia was going crazy about her art, so she wouldn't want to be bothered."

"Or you already knew she was dead," Amy suggested. "So, you knew there would be no point in contacting her."

"I had no idea she was dead," Lincoln said. "I didn't know until the next day when we were told we couldn't use the studio because it was a crime scene."

"Yes. It's a shame that you won't be able to work on your entry for the contest until the scene is cleared," said Heather. "With

Tricia out of the running, it must be easier for you to win."

"I don't care about winning that contest," Lincoln said. "Holiday art isn't really my thing, but I'm doing it because it's decent publicity for your other art."

"Wouldn't winning be better publicity?" Amy asked.

"I'm just saying I wasn't obsessed with winning like some of the others were. Tricia and Ray both wanted to win and were making the studio a hostile place to work," Lincoln said. "I just wanted to make my art and thought it wasn't a complete waste of time to enter the tree contest."

Amy rolled her eyes. It was possible that there was a new person she wanted to be the killer so that they could see him behind bars.

"How many people knew about you and Tricia?" Heather asked.

"I didn't know anyone knew," Lincoln said. "But we weren't being super secretive about it. I guess anyone at the studio could have known. Is there anything else you want to know?"

"That's all for now," Heather said. "We'll be in touch."

They walked away from his house, and Amy looked to her friend.

"He was her lover," Amy said. "And he's strong enough to have lifted her. Could he be the killer?"

"It's certainly a possibility," Heather said.

Chapter 13 – Hidden Clues

"It's weird coming back here," Amy said. "I mean I do want to come back here and take more classes and become a part of the Key West art community, but it also feels weird because the last time we were here we found a dead body."

"I understand what you mean," Heather assured her.

"I just don't like that it was supposed to be my new happy place and it became a crime scene," Amy continued.

"I know," Heather said. "But it will go back to being an art studio as soon as we crack the case. I'm sure that's what an artist like Tricia would have wanted: for the art to continue."

"Yeah. You're right," Amy said. "They should probably make an artistic tribute for her there when this is over. Some sort of art to commemorate her."

"That's a beautiful idea," Heather said.

"But with nothing to do with Christmas trees," Amy said definitively.

They were closer to the Sculpture Garden now and saw Ryan waving them over.

"But while this is still a crime scene, let's get to work," Heather said.

They hurried over to Ryan who looked almost cheerful.

"What did you find?" Heather asked when she saw his face.

"Now that I have found it, I'm almost embarrassed that I didn't see it before," Ryan said.

"Is it an optical illusion?" Amy asked.

"Maybe in a sense," Ryan said. "It was hiding in plain sight."

"What is it?" Heather asked. "A good clue?"

"What's different?" Ryan asked.

He gestured to the sculptures surrounding them. It looked the same as it had when they first visited it. There were large statues in different styles all around them. Amy moved closer to Kendall's statue and examined it.

"Some of these mirror pieces are broken now," Amy said.

"Right," said Ryan. "Something broke them."

"That's seven years bad luck,"
said Amy.

"Hopefully it is for the killer," Ryan
agreed.

"The murderer broke pieces of
the statue?" Heather asked. "But
why?"

"Follow me," Ryan said. He
moved past Kendall's sculpture
and further back among the
pieces until they were closer to
the statue that looked like a train.
It took Heather a moment to
realize what was different from
the first time they were there.

"The tracks," Heather said.

"Exactly," Ryan said. "There's a ladder laying on the train tracks. It was blending in so well that we didn't find it until now."

"That was smart," Amy said. "Any of the artists could have figured out this spot where your eye is tricked into ignoring it."

"It's a big ladder," Ryan said. "It would have been difficult for the killer to have taken it away from the studio with him without someone noticing. You'd notice someone traveling with something this tall late at night. And so, the killer decided to leave it here."

"But why hide it?" Heather asked. "It would have made sense for a studio to have a ladder? Does it change the dynamics of the crime?"

"Or the killer wanted to hide something incriminating that he left behind," Ryan said, pointing. There was some red paint on one of the steps, and it resembled a shoe print.

"Is that the same special holly red color that was found at the scene?" asked Heather.

Ryan nodded. "And that paint had to be spilled after Tricia was left alone at the studio. Everyone agreed that it wasn't spilled while they were there. So, it was either spilled by Tricia right before the killer arrived or it happened while the murder was being committed. Either way, this paint and this shoe print comes from our killer."

Heather was about to compliment Ryan on his find when they heard a phone ring. Heather and Ryan both reached for their phones, and they were both right. They smiled as they both answered their calls with "Shepherd."

Amy jokingly grumbled about how unpopular she was because nobody was calling her.

The Donut Delights – Key West business line was calling her. It was rare that they had a problem big enough to contact her about, so she was concerned until she heard Digby's reason for the call.

"Mr. Rankle brought over even more decorations for us to put up," Digby said. "There's a bunch more string Christmas lights and light-up stars and even a glowing reindeer. What should I do with them? I'm rooting for putting them in the trash."

Heather sighed. "I guess we should try and hang these up too."

"Are you sure?" Digby asked. "There's a lot."

"Do the best you can," Heather said. "Try to put it all up and try to make it look nice. But this might be our only chance keep goodwill with Mr. Rankle all year."

Digby reluctantly agreed. She hung up and turned to Ryan who said that Detective Peters had also found a clue. They moved away from the studio and down the street.

They saw Peters wearing gloves and a mask to cover his nose. He moved the mask to greet them and then showed them towards the trashcans she had been poking through.

"Gross," Amy said. "Please tell me it was worthwhile to go through the garbage."

"It was," Peters said. "And the killer made a mistake disposing of the evidence too."

"What evidence?" asked Heather.

"Rainboots," answered Peters. "I saw a boot on the ground near the trashcan. The killer must have been in a rush and wasn't paying proper attention. It fell out. I looked inside and found the other boot. And they both have the paint on it."

"The holly paint?" Amy asked.

"That's right," said Peters.

"That looked like a match to the print we found on the ladder steps," said Ryan. "The killer must have been wearing these boots that night."

"And," Heather said, remembering. "We talked to someone who was missing his favorite pair of shoes."

"It looks like we're not going to catch this killer red-handed," Amy said. "But we might be able to catch him red-footed."

Chapter 14 – The Side Studio

Kendall looked more downcast as she watched the artists work this time around. The small workroom was not as impressive as the other space and was a constant reminder why they were in a different place.

Heather, Amy, and Ryan had tracked Ray down to this small studio. Peters was bringing the new evidence to the station for closer examination, while the others went to question the artist about his boot prints.

Ray seemed to be making a garland out of fishing materials. Lucy and Kendall were also in the room. Lucy was creating pinwheels, and Kendall was either drawing a picture or plans on how to run her art classes in a new building.

"Thanks for coordinating this so we could still work," Lucy said.

"It was a good idea you had," Kendall said. "And I do need to start making plans for moving my classes around. People might not want to return to the studio knowing someone was killed there. This is going to be tough for business."

"Well, we won't be scared off," Lucy said. "We'll always support you. I'm sure Lincoln will too. He's very dedicated to his art."

"I know it's difficult for you to work here when the base of your sculptures and most of your materials are still in the studio," Kendall said. "I hope having this workspace helps a little."

Ray made a grunt of annoyance.

"We're very appreciative," Lucy said. "I hope some of the other decide to drop by."

They noticed the investigators and walked up to them. Ray continued working with his tackle box.

"What are you doing here?" Lucy asked. "I mean, did you solve the case?"

"We're following a lead," Heather said.

Kendall looked at Amy. "I should have invited you to come for the impromptu building session, but I thought you might have your hands full with investigating."

"You were right about that," Amy said.

"If you'll excuse us," Ryan said. "We'd like to speak with Ray for a moment."

"Why me?" Ray asked.

"We'd like to talk to you about shoes," Heather said.

"Shoes?" Ray asked.

"Yeah," Amy said. "We want to know if the shoe fits."

Ray followed them outside of the room with a slight hobble and giving them a suspicious eye the whole time.

"What's this about shoes?" he asked.

"You told us that you were missing your favorite pair," Heather said.

"And based on the way you're walking, you're still wearing those too small shoes you didn't like."

"So?" Ray asked.

"Can you describe your favorite shoes?" Heather asked.

"Sure," Ray said. "They're rainboots. They were real comfy, and it didn't matter if they got dirty or you spilled paint or stuff on them. They were gray and had a strap on the side."

"That sounds like a match," Ryan said. He showed Ray a picture of the shoes they had found in the garbage down the street from the crime scene. "Are these your boots?"

"You found them!" Ray said. "Those are mine, but I don't

remember getting anything red on them. Still, when can I get them back?"

"After they're no longer evidence in a murder case," Ryan said.

"In the murder case," Ray repeated, growing pale. "That is paint on them, right? It ain't blood?"

"It is paint," Heather started.

"Good," Ray said, exhaling. "I don't do well with blood. Especially when you know it's blood from a dead person."

"Horatio said he didn't do well with blood," Amy mentioned. "Or his wife told us on his behalf."

"Just the thought of blood makes me feel queasy," Ray said.

"It's not blood," Heather reiterated. "But it is paint and a very specific paint. It's the special red paint that you ordered for your statue. And it was spilled the night of the murder."

"My Holly Berry Jam Red?" Ray asked. "That figures. Tricia must have stolen it when she stayed late that night."

"Why would she steal your paint?" asked Ryan.

"She was always stealing my things – my materials, my ideas. She was doing it again this year. She was planning on making a boating-themed Christmas tree when she knew I was making a fishing themed one," Ray fumed. "There was bound to be cross-over in our designs."

"And is that why you stole her propeller?" Heather asked.

"No. I stole it because," Ray started. "I mean, I never said I stole it."

"You kinda just did," Amy said.

"And we saw the propeller in your yard," Heather said.

"Fine," Ray said. "What she accused me of that day was true. It was me that stole her propeller, but that's because she stole my idea and my rainboots."

"You think Tricia stole your boots?" asked Heather.

"Well, who else would do it?" Ray asked. "She didn't like me, and she was a thief."

"Maybe you just misplaced them?" Amy suggested. "Or you used them to kill somebody and then got rid of them?"

"No," Ray said. "My rainboots were missing two days before she died. You didn't see me in boots when you came to that art session, did you?"

"I guess not," Heather said.

"I think we would have noticed rainboots inside a building on a sunny day," Amy agreed.

"But that doesn't mean that they were missing," Heather said. "You could have chosen not to wear them."

"They were missing for two days, and I thought Tricia took them to be spiteful. That's why I took her propeller," Ray said. "And since I'm admitting that I can tell you that I didn't go out drinking the night she died. I was adding the propeller quick to a statue in my yard. I was trying to hide it."

"Why didn't you just get rid of it?" asked Amy.

"Because I wanted to use it in my tree," Ray said. "Tricia was right about that. It would look cool as part of the design. And I thought it was fitting for me to use her idea after she tried to steal mine twice."

"Did anyone see you at home that night attaching the propeller?" Ryan asked.

"My one neighbor did come out and yell at me at some point,"

Ray said. "He said I was being too loud at night."

"We'll check on that," Ryan said.

"I didn't kill anybody," Ray said. "And since I told you about taking the propeller already, I guess I can tell you something else. It might be a clue."

Chapter 15 – The Note

Ray led them back into the room and picked up his jacket by his art project.

"What's going on?" Lucy asked. "Is he a suspect?"

"I won't be after I show them this," Ray said, going through his pockets.

Kendall and Lucy hurried closer to Ray as well as the investigators. Ray found what he was looking for and handed the crumpled note to Heather.

"This was with the propeller when I took it. It must have gotten stuck on it when I got it out of the studio," he said.

"You did take her propeller?" Kendall said. "I was telling her that is must have been some sort of accident because our artists wouldn't do something so dishonest."

Ray shrugged. "She kept stealing my ideas. And she went too far when she took my shoes."

"We don't know that she took your shoes," Heather said.

"What does the note say?" Amy asked.

"It says: You can't do this!"
Heather said.

"It's a shame we won't be able to get any prints off of it," Ryan said. "But with Ray moving and crumpling it, I don't think we'll be able to recover anything."

"That might not be necessary," Kendall said. "I think I recognize that handwriting. It's Lincoln's, isn't it?"

Lucy shrugged. "I don't know. It's hard to tell. It might be anyone's."

Kendall collected her bag and took out a sign-up sheet from one of her classes. Lincoln's name and contact information was written on it, and the shape of the letters matched perfectly. Both the note and his signature had the same wavy loops.

"That's a match," Ryan said.

"But it couldn't have been Lincoln who killed her," Lucy said. "Everyone knows he has band practice right after our sessions, and they go on all night."

"The drummer was sick," Heather said. "They had to end early."

"You can't keep jamming without someone keeping the beat," Amy said.

"I think it's time we had another chat with Lincoln," said Ryan.

***

Lincoln opened the door and didn't like seeing the private investigators joined by a detective.

"Something tells me that you're not here to buy demo tape of Lincoln and the Loggers," he said.

"No," Ryan said. "We're here to talk more about Tricia Mollins."

"I didn't kill her," Lincoln said. "I was seeing her sort of. But, like I said before, it was casual. And I didn't see her after I left that night."

"We've come across some new information," Heather said. "A note you left for her."

"Is this your handwriting?" Ryan asked, showing him the paper.

"Yeah," Lincoln said. "And I wrote it, but it doesn't have anything to do with her murder."

"What are you telling her she can't do?" asked Heather.

"You added an exclamation point to it," Amy said. "That makes it look more dramatic and angrier."

"It's nothing," said Lincoln.

Ryan said, "It looks like you were having a fight with your lover, and because she was found dead soon after you wrote this, it's not nothing."

"I wrote that a few days before she died," Lincoln said.

Heather had to admit that the timing tracked. The note needed to be stuck to the propeller that Ray stole from the studio a day or two before the more murderous crime.

"But what were you upset about?" Heather asked.

"I was just telling her not to go through with a stupid idea of hers. She wanted to take Ray's special paint to annoy him because she said that he kept stealing her ideas. I left the note near her materials so she wouldn't try and take his stuff while I wasn't there. I knew it would get her into trouble," Lincoln said. "Though I didn't think it would be that much trouble."

"You think stealing the paint was what led to her death?" asked Ryan.

"It makes as much sense as anything else," said Lincoln. "If I knew this tree competition was going to be so deadly, I never would have gotten involved."

"He just doesn't seem upset enough about this death," Amy said. "The lady he was dating was just murdered, and he's being very indifferent about it."

"I'm not indifferent. I'd rather she was alive than dead," said Lincoln. "But there's nothing I can do about it now."

"See, that still doesn't seem sincerely sad," said Amy.

"And he doesn't have a great alibi," Heather said to the others.

Lincoln didn't like being talked about while he was in the room and jumped at the bait. He started talking. "I don't have a great alibi, but if I did kill her, don't you think I would have tried and gotten a better one? I could have gone back to meet some of my band members and tricked them about how long I was gone."

"See what he came up with?" Amy said. "He does have a criminal mind."

"Look," Lincoln said. "How was she supposed to have been killed?"

"We were thinking that someone could have been strong enough to throw her onto the sharp points," Heather said.

"Then I couldn't have done it," Lincoln said.

"You have big arm muscles," Amy said.

"Yeah. But strained one of them last week. I've tried to hide it, so people don't notice I'm not making certain movements. But it hurts if I extend my left arm up to high. I tried a dance move at a band practice and hurt it. My bandmates can back me up. It's been bad all week," Lincoln said.

"Adrenaline could have helped you move it," Amy said.

"And there is a ladder to consider now too," said Heather.

"I didn't kill her," Lincoln said. "You have to believe me."

"We have to follow the evidence where it leads us," said Ryan.

"And right now, it's telling us it was someone from the studio," said Heather.

Chapter 16 – A Bright Idea

"There's certainly no shortage of holiday cheer here," Heather said.

"I'm practically blinded by it," Amy said, dramatically shielding her eyes.

"As long as there are good donuts here, the décor doesn't really matter," Eva said.

"And now the store looks like a shining beacon of deliciousness," Leila said.

They were sitting at the ladies' usual table a Donut Delights and were enjoying the Spiced Maple Donuts more than overpowering light display. After they had hung up all the many decorations that Mr. Rankle had given them, the store was overflowing. All the flat surfaces that were not being used to bake or house donuts were covered with light-up poinsettias and shiny stars.

Amy pulled a pair of sunglasses out of her bag and put them on. "I don't know," she said. "Maybe we were better off being enemies with Mr. Rankle. It was better for my eyes."

"Come now," Eva said. "We don't want to be enemies with anyone at Christmastime."

"Except for maybe with the killer," Leila said. "But not in a he's chasing you sort of way. And more in a we don't want to be friends with a killer sort of way."

"I really hope it wasn't Kendall," Amy said. "Though I don't think it was. Those pictures of her destructive dog help give an alibi. And he is destructive. Much worse behaved than Miss Marshmallow."

The other women exchanged a look. Amy was becoming fonder of her foster dog.

"What?" asked Amy, eyeing them all.

"Nothing," Heather said quickly.

"If it's not Kendall," Eva started.

"And her business might suffer because of this. And she's been so nice to me, and believed in my art," Amy said. "I don't think it's her."

"I'm sure you're right," Eva said. "But if it's not her, who do you think did it?"

"It could be any of the artists," Heather said.

"The victim was killed on Horatio's statue, the boot prints were from Ray, and that note was from Lincoln," Amy recapped.

"I think that Horatio's statue was used because it was pointy and provided an opportunity for the murder," Heather said. "But I don't think he was planning for it."

"Not after we saw that pretty design he drew for how the tree was supposed to end up looking," said Amy.

Heather nodded. "I don't really think he's involved. But Ray still could be. It depends on whether we believe him that his boots were stolen."

"If he's lying, then he used them for the murder and came up with a cover story to explain why they're gone," Amy said. "But if he's telling the truth, then somebody used his boots to try and frame him."

"And it would be a convincing frame," said Heather. "He and Tricia were constantly bickering and accusing one another of theft."

"And that paint was his," Amy said.

"Right," said Heather. "That paint made sure that the boot prints were left and that we knew the prints happened at the time of the murder."

"But then why did the killer get rid of the evidence?" Amy asked.

"Wouldn't he have wanted us to find the print right away?"

"The ladder and the boots were hidden, but they weren't impossible to find. One boot was even outside of the trashcan," said Heather. "I think the killer wanted us to think that we had worked hard to find those clues, but it's possible that he wanted them to be found."

"So, who would want to frame this man?" asked Eva.

"It might be because he was the most likely suspect and not against him personally," said Heather.

"That might make sense," said Amy. "Because why would the boot print need to be on the ladder? Why would the killer climb the ladder? To drop the victim from higher up?"

"I think you might have hit on something," Heather said, thinking. "There is something strange about this ladder."

She picked up another donut as she began to chew her thoughts. She was so deep in this concentration that she almost didn't notice when Detective Peters popped into the shop.

"Hi Heather," he said.

"Hi. Do you have any news on the case?" asked Heather.

"No," Peters said, blushing. "I thought I would just stop by and get some donuts on a break."

"A good idea," said Heather, though she suspected that the real reason he had decided to stop in was to see her pretty red-headed assistant that he has a crush on. "I'm afraid Janae won't be able to help you at the counter tonight. She switched shifts so she could lead a bike tour."

"Oh, that's all right," Peters said, covering his disappointment with machismo. "I didn't come to see her specifically. Not that I don't like her serving me. Serving me donuts, not serving me. But I came just for the food."

Heather nodded and headed with him to the counter where Digby was squinting at them to block out some of the bright lights.

Before Detective Peters could make his order, he was interrupted by Mr. Rankle's appearance on the scene. Heather started to thank him for all his gracious decorations, but he ignored her and went right up to Peters.

"Officer, do your duty and shut down this shop," he demanded.

"What?" Peters asked, looking completely taken aback.

"According to local town ordinance 77-25C, there is a limit on how bright Christmas light decorations can be in a business setting. Looking around, you can see that this is a clear violation of the ordinance," Mr. Rankle said.

"Talk about a snake in the pear tree," Amy said, glaring at him.

"Officer, this display is an eyesore for the town and can negatively affect business for the whole area with its blatant disregard for retinal safety."

"We didn't know about this ordinance," Heather said.

"That's right," Mr. Rankle said. "As an out-of-towner trying to whittle your way into our holiday business, you wouldn't know anything about our important town ordinances. Unfortunately, ignorance of the law is no excuse. Officer, you'll have to hold them responsible."

"What do you want me to do?" Peters asked.

"According to the law, they could be charged a hefty fine for this monstrosity. Or the business can be shut down until the display is removed. Shut them down," Mr. Rankle said.

"But just until the display is down?" asked Peters.

"Or indefinitely," Mr. Rankle suggested.

"This is unfair," Amy said. "The only reason we have up so many decorations is because Mr. Rankle donated them to us and we were trying to be nice. We should have realized it was a trick."

"A trick," Heather said, getting an idea.

"That's right," Digby said. "I certainly wouldn't have chosen a decorative scheme like this. It's way too bright."

"It is rather bright," Peters said.

"I can fix that though," said Amy.

She walked over to the outlet and removed the lights' plugs. It was instantly darker and looked more like a normal shop.

"I think that fixes it for now," said Peters. "And if I was just supposed to shut you down until you take down the excess décor, well, it's only an hour until closing time. You'll have this all fixed by the time you open tomorrow, right?"

"Right," Amy said.

"Fine," Digby said.

"Tricia was tricked," Heather was muttering to herself. "She was lulled into a false sense of security. And maybe she was the one on the ladder."

"You're not going to shut them down?" Mr. Rankle asked, looking crestfallen. "But they were breaking the law."

"An ordinance," Amy clarified.

"And they're about to fix things," Peters said. "No harm. No foul."

He selected a donut and then left the shop.

"I don't know," Amy muttered. "I think there might be something foul here."

"What a nasty trick," Eva said.

"Very Grinch-like," Eva agreed.

Mr. Rankle didn't have anything he wanted to say to them and marched out of the store angrily.

"The joke is doubly on him because he ended up paying for all these decorations," Amy said.

"Should we use some of them on our house?"

"Some of them," Eva said. "We don't need all the lights."

"That's right," said Leila. "We do want to be able to sleep at night."

"But who could have convinced Tricia to get on the ladder?" Heather was saying. "And what could the motive be?"

Suddenly, a thought occurred to Heather. Her face lit up like the string lights had before.

"Do we really need to take down all these decorations tonight?" Digby asked.

"Yes," Heather said. "And I'm afraid I have more bad news. You and Luz will have to take them down by yourselves. Amy and I have to go. Do you think we can catch up with Peters?"

"Did you just solve the case?" Amy asked.

"I think so," said Heather.

Chapter 17 – Artist Gathering

"Thanks for gathering everyone together," Heather told Kendall.

"I was happy too, but I don't really see how it will help," she admitted.

"You will," said Amy.

They had assembled all the artists from the night of the murder in the small space that Kendall was using until they could return to the studio. She had called the meeting under the guise of creating a memorial art piece for Tricia. Kendall had told Amy that she really did think the memorial was a wonderful idea, but she knew that the real reason for gathering them was to flush out a murderer.

"Here we go," Heather said.

She and Amy strode into the room, followed by Kendall. They faced the other artists.

"What's going on?" Lucy asked.

"I thought we were going to work on a memorial for Tricia," Lincoln said.

"Is this some kind of setup?" asked Ray.

Horatio didn't say anything.

"We're sorry to interrupt your meeting," Heather said. "But we wanted to get here before the police did."

"They'll be here any minute," Amy said. "They said that they figured out who the killer is and they're going to arrest him."

"Him?" Ray said, taking note of the two women in the room.

"We just wanted to let you know that if you confess, the court will be more lenient on you," said Heather.

"Which is good because it looks like this case will go up against the most ruthless judge, and he doesn't like it when ladies are killed," said Amy. "So, it would be in your best interest to confess."

"Are you sure it was one of them?" Kendall asked.

"The police are sure," said Heather. "They said they have an airtight case and that they're prepared to ask for the maximum sentence."

"It's pretty certain they'll get it too," said Amy.

"Good," Lucy said. "No one should get away with murder."

They heard footsteps in the hallway.

"Last chance," Amy said, but no one took her up on the offer.

Ryan and Detective Peters came in and somberly moved towards Lincoln.

"Wait," he said. "I didn't do it."

"We had the note analyzed," Peters said.

"It's an open and shut case," said Ryan.

"No," Lincoln said. "It wasn't me."

"Lincoln Conner, you have the right to remain silent," Ryan began.

"No," Lucy said, piping up and running towards them. "It wasn't him. It was me. I did it."

"Lucy?" Lincoln asked.

"Why couldn't you have just stayed at band practice like you were supposed to?" Lucy asked. "You were going to have the perfect alibi. They should never have suspected you."

"But why did you do it?" Lincoln asked.

"Why?" asked Lucy. "Because I loved you. And you would never notice me as long as Tricia was around. But with her out of the picture, you might have chosen me. I would have been so good for you. I'd kill for you."

"I never asked for that!" said Lincoln.

"I don't want you to get blamed for what I did," Lucy said. "They were supposed to think Ray did it. That's why I took his boots."

"She took my boots! Did you hear that?" Ray asked. "Arrest her."

"Yeah. I think they're going to," Amy said.

"I love you," Lucy said to Lincoln. "I just wanted you to notice me."

Ryan and Peters read Lucy her rights and led her out of the room. Lincoln had to take a seat. Horatio and Ray exchanged a look.

"I guess this meeting is over then?" Ray asked.

Kendall nodded. "The reconvene to discuss Tricia's memorial. I want to talk to these investigators some more."

The other artists started to head out, but Kendall stayed to talk.

"I bet there was nothing new about that note," Kendall said. "You knew it was Lucy all along."

"I was pretty sure," Heather said.

"But how?" asked Kendall.

"Because of the ladder," Heather said. "Once we realized a ladder was involved in the crime, it changed things. The killer no longer had to be tall and strong. It could have been a small woman. Lucy convinced Tricia to climb on the ladder and then pushed her so that she fell to her death."

"But couldn't any of them have done that?" asked Kendall.

"I started to think about who Tricia would have climbed the ladder for," Heather said. "Lucy was short, so if she asked Tricia to climb up and help her add something to her tall tree, it wouldn't have seemed suspicious."

"And Lucy's tree was next to Horatio's," said Amy. "She asked for help on hers, but pushed her onto the next one."

"The boots missing made me think that it was premeditated," said Heather. "The killer had made some preparations for this crime so that she could blame someone else for it."

"And if it was premeditated," Amy said. "The killer should have come up with a better alibi for himself."

"That's right. I thought about how Lincoln almost had a perfect alibi, but how he changed his plans at the last minute," said Heather. "That didn't seem like the work of a premeditating murderer."

"But maybe someone trying to protect Lincoln would have used the opportunity to kill when she knew that he would have an alibi," said Amy.

"As soon as I realized that I thought about how often Lucy mentioned Lincoln," said Heather. "She was in love with him."

"She thought that we wouldn't suspect her of a physical murder because of her size, and she hoped we'd blame Ray," said Heather. "He and Tricia had a history of fighting, and she tried to frame him by using his boots."

"And that's why there was red paint from the boot on the ladder," said Heather. "The killer didn't need to stand on the ladder. Lucy just wanted to leave several prints from the man she was trying to frame that night." "I'm glad you were on the case," said Kendall. "Otherwise, I bet she would have gotten away with it."

"Killers usually make one mistake," said Heather. "Hers

was protecting Lincoln's alibi instead of her own."

"There's only one more thing that we need to figure out," Kendall said, smiling. "And that's what art classes you want to take."

"Well, it might sound crazy," Amy said. "But I have been thinking about that."

Chapter 18 – Donut Delights Decorations

"It's beautiful," Eva said.

"Lovely," agreed Leila.

"And much better than the Rankle display," said Digby.

They all chuckled.

"It really is wonderful," Heather said to her bestie. "Thank you."

They were all admiring the new decorative display at Donut Delights. They had taken down the overabundance of lights from Mr. Rankle and now only had a few tasteful ones up. In the center of the window now though was Amy's contribution.

She had been working with Kendall to create her own sculpture and had made a Christmas tree statue for display. This one had no pointy parts on it and was decorated with colorful circular ornaments that were reminiscent of donuts.

"It's perfect," Heather said. "And I'm glad that you found something that could be your own thing."

"And I'm glad that it still fits in with all the other things in my life that I love."

The two friends hugged.

"Some of those donut decorations look good enough to eat," Leila said.

"Don't," Eva said, handing her friend a sugary donut instead.

"Is everything all right?" Amy said, looking Heather. "Have I been ignoring you too much?"

"No," Heather said. "And everything is good. The shop is doing well, we caught the killer, and these decorations look great. I'm also excited for Christmas, and while I still need to figure out the perfect gift for Lilly, I have time."

"But?"

"But I guess I am little disappointed about Mr. Rankle," she admitted. "I thought he was finally coming around and he wasn't. He's still the same old grouch he is every other time of the year."

"Who knows?" Amy said as they looked out the window and at the other shops on the street. "Maybe he will get into the Christmas spirit and suddenly become a kinder, gentler old man like Scrooge becomes after his magical night."

Mr. Rankle seemed to sense that he was being watched and shook his fist for good measure before re-entering his shop. They could have sworn they heard him say, "Bah humbug."

Heather and Amy laughed.

The End.

A letter from the Author

To each and every one of my Amazing readers: *I hope you enjoyed this story as much as I enjoyed writing it. Let me know what you think by leaving a review!*

Stay Curious,
Susan Gillard

58194480R00126

Made in the USA
Middletown, DE
19 December 2017